# Barnaby Bennett

TO JACK A. RAT - PICK OF THE PACK. AROHANUI HANNAH
FOR JOHNNY, LOVE ALI

First Published in 2006 by Huia Publishers, New Zealand.
Published in 2009 in the United States of America by Star Bright Books, Inc.,
30-19 48th Avenue, Long Island City, NY 11101.

The name Star Bright Books and the Star Bright Books logo are registered
trademarks of Star Bright Books, Inc. Please visit www.starbrightbooks.com.
For bulk orders, please email orders@starbrightbooks.com

ISBN-13:  978-1-59572-156-3
Printed in China (C&C)  9 8 7 6 5 4 3 2 1

Library of Congress Cataloging-in-Publication Data

Rainforth, Hannah, 1976-
  Barnaby Bennett / by Hannah Rainforth ; illustrated by Ali Teo.
     p. cm.
  Summary: Barnaby Bennett has decided to wear only red, but his strong will is soon matched
  by his strong odor, and his family members strive to convince him to wear something else.
  ISBN 978-1-59572-156-3 (pbk. : alk. paper)
  [1. Stories in rhyme. 2. Clothing and dress–Fiction. 3. Cleanliness–Fiction. 4. Family life–Fiction.]
  I. Teo, Ali, ill. II. Title.
  PZ8.3.R14483Bar 2008
  [E]–dc22
                                        2008039733

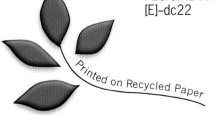
Printed on Recycled Paper

# Barnaby Bennett

by **HANNAH RAINFORTH**

illustrated by **ALI TEO**

"I'm *Barnaby Bennett*,"
Barnaby said.

"I'm *Barnaby Bennett*!"
He leapt out of bed.

"I've had an epiphany,
I've had an idea.
I've decided that red
is all I will wear."

He rummaged, scrummaged,
searched here and there
**for red red red red**
all the red he could wear.

Hauled out his jammies

YANKED on his socks

**grabbed his aunt's scarf**

from out of a box.

He sneaked in and borrowed
his brother's red slippers
left in their place
his best-ever
flippers

When he had gathered a
# GINORMOUS pile,
he grinned a big grin
and dressed up in style.

He **wore them** to **school**
**wore them** to **bed**
for weeks upon weeks
**wore nothing but red.**

But his red clothes got dirty
**grubby** and **smudged**
**muddy** and **spluddy**
and covered in

"Oh Barnaby, Barnaby,"
Sissy Girl mumbled.
"Wear something else.
You're dirty," she grumbled.

"Like **yellow?**" he asked.
"Or do you mean **green?**

**I certainly won't.**
I'd look like a bean."

"I'm Barnaby Bennett," Barnaby said.

"I'm Barnaby Bennett, I only wear red."

"**Pooh-pooh** to the **blue**," Barnaby said.

"I'm *Barnaby Bennett.* **I only wear red.**"

**"Bro,"** said his bro,
"I'll give you my hat
if you wear something else.
Now what about that?"

"That thing?" said Barnaby.
"But that thing is yellow."
"I'll never, not ever,
no, never wear
**yellow.**"

Then his aunt came by.
Her hair went all stiff.
Her nose stood on end.
Oh, the stink and the whiff.

"I'll fix this!" she cried.
Off she went home.
She shut her front door.
She turned off the phone.

Out came the scissors,
the bobbins, the thread.
"Right!" she exclaimed.
"Enough of this red!"

Zip zip she zapped up
a wondrous creation.
Great nifty sewing-
oh what innovation.

It had **pockets** galore,
a **dinosaur hood**,
**mechanical tail**
and claws made of wood.

It had **sherbet supplies,**
and **built-in marshmallows.**
And from bottom to top
was **utterly yellow.**

**"Will he wear it?"** she asked.
"Only one way to tell.
I certainly hope so –
I can't stand his smell."

He saw it. He frowned.
**"Yellow?"** he said.
"I'm *Barnaby Bennett.*
**I only wear red."**

But he looked and looked,
thought for a while,
**"Now, this isn't red."**
Then said with a smile,

said with a **whoop,**
said with a **bellow,**
"And now I'll only,
yes always, wear ...